Jonathan's Locket

Lorraine Carey

Jonathan's Locket

Dedication

Jonathan's Locket is dedicated to the brave men and women of Grand Cayman, who risked their lives and came to the rescue of the victims of the Wreck of the Ten Sails in 1794 off the east end of the island.

The Wreck of the Ten Sails is a true account. The rest of the story is entirely fiction.

Acknowledgements

The many times my husband dove into the crystal clear waters off Grand Cayman, he would vividly describe the treasures he saw. It was his love for the magic of the sea that inspired me to tell this tale. I would like to thank him for his knowledge, guidance, and support during the creation of Jonathan's Locket.

Chapters

Chapter 1

1794 Port Royal Jamaica

Jonathan Palmer tossed and turned in his bed. He couldn't help but anticipate the adventure that awaited him in the wee hours of the morning. The gleam of moonlight that streamed through his window only added to his feeling of restlessness.

He jumped out of bed to pick up his antique pocket watch from the bedside table. It was four o'clock in the morning, and it was almost time for his final departure from the world he had known for some fifteen years. Soon, the years he spent at The Angelican House for boys would just be a memory.

He had it planned for months now. Nothing was going to stop him. He was ready to find his birthmother and learn the truth of his story, not the one told by the Sisters at the orphanage. Deep within his heart, he knew there was a strange secret they were hiding. Jonathan was ready to risk his life to uncover the truth.

He quickly dressed, pulling on his faded dungarees and pea coat. It was a chilly day in February, even for Jamaica. When he pulled on his favorite wool cap, caramel colored hair jutted out like pieces of straw. He grabbed his duffle sack, packed to the gills, and reached for the special locket that was kept in the top drawer of his chest. He carefully slipped the locket around his neck.

Jonathan tiptoed over to Marcus and Julian, who slept in the bunks across from him. Goodbye old buddies. I will pray for you as you will pray for me. I will never forget all of the great times that we shared together. Marcus and Julian did not wake. Jonathan wanted to slip away silently in the night. He especially did not want to wake Sister Mary Katherine – for she would surely thwart his well-planned escape.

As he tiptoed down the creaky wooden stairs, his duffel bag slung over his shoulder, he took one last peek into the old schoolroom. Jonathan froze in the doorway before snapping back to reality. Some of the better memories flashed through his head.

He remembered all the times he and Marcus would pretend to be ill and sneak down to the pier to go fishing. Of course they released the fish they caught, since they could not explain their finds to the Sisters.

One of his better memories was at Christmas time, when some of the wealthy families would deliver gifts to the boys. Somehow they knew exactly what they wanted.

When he as a small boy, he remembered receiving twice as many gifts as the other boys, though he could never understand why. He always let Marcus and Julian pick two of his presents.

Despite those memories, he knew that it was time to move on. He walked five blocks from the Angelican House at a brisk pace, until he reached the docks at Port Royal. It was time for his adventure to begin.

* * * * *

Jonathan knew the docks like the back of his hand. This was thanks to Peter Miller, a middle-aged seaman who was like a father to him. He had let Jonathan help load the ships since he was nine-years-old. Peter was a vital part of Jonathan's plan to escape.

As Jonathan approached the docks, he found himself mesmerized by the early morning sunrise as it glistened upon the water. He couldn't help but stare at the sky, ablaze with red streaks. An older seaman startled him from behind, grabbing him hard on the shoulder.

"Red sky at morning, sailor take warning," he declared. "This could be the sign of a rough start, son."

The sea was choppy, and Jonathan could see the whitecaps splashing their foam across the sea with great fury. The boy had never been at sea before. He had never gone further than the docks.

"And just what are you doing here, young man?" the older seaman asked.

"I am here to bid a friend goodbye."

Jonathan's heart hammered in his chest, as he silently prayed the seaman would believe his story. If he or Peter were to be caught for this, both would face dire consequences.

Jonathan took another look out at the rough seas, worrying He had heard other sailors speak of severe seasickness. He hoped not to experience this affliction. He assured himself that even if he did get sick, it would be worth the journey. He simply had to find his real mother and know how he mysteriously arrived at the orphanage. Though he pulled his pea coat tightly around his body, he still felt an eerie chill run through his veins.

I've got to hurry and get onto that ship before Captain Lawford and his men arrive, he thought.

Jonathan's plan was to hide aboard the British Royal Navy ship, the Convert. This ship would lead nine other merchant ships that were carrying cotton, rum, and wood to Britain.

He thought of finally finding his birthmother, as he swiftly snuck down into the inner hold of the ship. His heart raced with nervous anticipation. Peter had already instructed him of where to hide once he made it onto the ship. It was a comfort knowing that Peter would also be on board for the journey.

As Jonathan crept down into the hold, he could smell the musty air and the sweet smell of rum that wafted throughout the inner deck.

I hope I can find the trunk Peter told me to hide in, he thought nervously

Most of the trunks in the hold were filled with cotton, rum, sugar, and wood. Since there wasn't room on some of the other merchant ships, the Convert had agreed to carry some of their cargo. The rest of the ships were also loaded with the goods that Jamaica was shipping out.

Jonathan made his way in and out of the countless rows of old wooden trunks, desperately searching for the one he was to hide in. After looking through dozens of trunks, he finally found an empty one.

He slipped inside the large cedar trunk, pulled a blanket over the top, and closed the lid. There was thankfully a lot of room in the chest, as he was considered quite short for a boy of fifteen. Peter had promised to leave him a bag of ginger biscuits to quell his stomach in case he got seasick.

As he settled in, Jonathan opened his locket. Inside was a lock of dark blonde hair. He had been told long ago that it belonged to his mother. It was all that he had of her.

Jonathan had a reoccurring dream of being a small child and playing on a large grassy lawn on the grounds of a huge plantation house. A beautiful lady dressed in a long white gown would chase him across the grass. He remembered laughing and feeling blissfully happy. Somehow, he could never remember her face.

Each time he awoke, he hoped it had been his mother in the dream. If he did not have one in real life, at least he had her in his sleep.

"Convert Party - band your wares and begin to board immediately!" ordered a very loud Captain Lawford.

Jonathan lay quietly in the chest and listened to the buzz that went on around him. He had found the bag of biscuits that Peter had left him, but there was nothing to drink. Already he was feeling hot and thirsty being locked up in the trunk. He considered breaking into one of the other chests for rum if Peter did not show up in time, even though he knew that Peter would not forget about him.

* * * * *

Up on deck, Captain Lawford shouted directions in a booming voice. "Aye, all captains, ready your men for boarding your gangways! Grab those duffels, and if you have a Ditty Box, it is your responsibility. All Captains must show your Binnacle

List at the time of boarding. Each ship shall report its Clean Bill of Health to the port captain and keep on board."

All of the seamen and Captains quickly boarded in order of the lineup of each of the ships. All ears were on Captain Lawford as he issued orders.

Jonathan of course could not hear the commotion as he was sealed quite snugly in his trunk.

"We sail at 0600. The Convert shall be in the lead, followed by the other merchant ships: William and Elizabeth, the Moorhall, the Ludlow, the Britannia, the Richard, the Nancy, the Eagle, the Sally, and the Fortune."

Once the ships were boarded, the Union Jack was raised on the Convert. Everyone aboard pledged their allegiance to the royal flag.

"Weigh Anchor!"

While Jonathan hid, Peter stood on deck waiting for the traditional boarding ceremonies to finish. He grew anxious for the boarding protocol to end.

I need to sneak down into the inner hold to release that poor boy from his temporary confinement, he mused. God help me if they find out I have helped this boy stow away. Peter wasn't just worried about Jonathan, though. He also worried about the condition of the rough seas ahead. Unknowingly, he had put himself and Jonathan right into the path of serious danger.

Chapter 2

Scuttlebutt

Jonathan opened the lid of his trunk. Above him, it sounded like thousands of cattle were pounding their hooves. The seamen scurried to their assigned duties, while Jonathan was left wondering exactly what was happening. He hoped that Peter would come for him soon, for he couldn't fight that gnawing feeling in the pit of his stomach for much longer.

Up on deck Peter listened with apt attention as the duties were assigned to the newer seamen. Peter had easily been able to secure cargo hold watch. He was a long respected seaman who had been called upon many times to sail with Captain Lawford. This ensured that he could stay with Jonathan and make sure he was hidden. Two other seamen were also assigned to Cargo Hold watch. He still hadn't figured out how he would stop the pair from discovering Jonathan.

Peter thought about all the years he had known of Jonathan's tragic birth story and kept it a secret. He wanted Jonathan to have a stable father figure in his life….at times he felt as though he owed it to Jonathan to protect him.

Finally, Peter was able to get down to the trunk where Jonathan was hidden.

"Jonathan, Jonathan!" Peter whispered hoarsely.

Quickly, Jonathan opened the trunk and climbed out. He sprinted into Peter's familiar arms, glad to be reunited with a familiar face.

"I am so glad you came," Jonathan said, breathless.

"I couldn't forget about you, good buddy," Peter replied. "Did you get the biscuits?"

"I did, but I am so thirsty that I was ready to hit the rum," Jonathan quipped.

"Oh, my dear boy, you are a bit too young for that stuff," laughed Peter. "I will bring you some flasks of water soon. I have to check all the cargo down here and report to my officer in command. I will be back in an hour or two. Remember, when I am not here, two other seamen will be down here doing their inspections. You must stay hidden from them. Either stay inside the trunk or behind some of the crates in the corner. If they find you Jonathan, we will both be in serious trouble!"

"I will do everything I can to protect us both, Peter. I know how much you have sacrificed to get me out of Jamaica."

Peter looked straight into Jonathan's dark blue eyes. He could see that they were full of gratitude and hope for the future. Since Peter had met the young boy all those years ago, he had come to understand the emptiness that lingered inside of him. Jonathan had spent too many days desperate for answers. Peter always felt protective of the boy. He was glad for the chance to help him – even if it put them both at risk.

Jonathan watched Peter go about his duties. He checked each trunk in the cargo hold to make sure that they were fastened tightly. Peter's tall, lanky body bent over each trunk as he tied the ropes into knots. Peter was only in his mid-thirties, but he looked far older than his age. Jonathan studied the thick streaks of grey that peppered his long hair.

Jonathan was only somewhat aware that Peter had a rough past. You would never know it from his kind heart.

Peter, being an orphan, had mostly grown up on the streets. A local family would take him in now and then, but he would only find himself in the company of strangers who had problems of their own.

As a teenager, Peter had gotten involved with some smugglers who had him doing their dirty bidding by offering him food and a place to sleep on an old ship.

One evening, as Peter was returning from a delivery job, he had noticed their ship was not in the docks. Instinctively he knew that his providers must have sensed they were in trouble and left for another port.

This is why Peter had enlisted at the port as a long shoreman at the age of sixteen.

"Listen, my boy," Peter started, "there is Scuttlebutt abound, as the seas ahead are supposed to be even rougher than we thought. We are taking the route to the western tip of Cuba and then through the Florida Channel. We should reach the southern tip of Cuba by late evening, at 1900 hours."

"I remember hearing about this trade route from the other seamen," added Jonathan.

"We should lead some of the other ships to the Florida Straits and off to Britain and reach the Florida Straits in a few days," Peter continued.

After a few moments he said, "I've heard the men talking about an old witch from Jamaica. They had warned them that the sirens of the sea would be out in these waters, especially with the full moon. Don't worry though, I know it is just scuttle-but. Old sailors love to spin yarns.

There is also talk of Royalty being aboard one of the ships. Of course they don't usually say which one, since they are highly guarded."

"I heard lots of those stories at the docks, but never the ones about the sirens," said Jonathan. He pondered the concept for a brief moment. "Just what are sirens?"

"They are an ancient Greek myth about evil mermaids of the sea who lure sailors into the waters to steal their souls," Peter answered. "In all my years of sailing, I have never known anyone who had seen them. The legend claims that their singing voices drive the men mad, and the only relief from the madness is to jump ship."

"Will we encounter any pirates?" asked Jonathan. There was a touch of fear in his voice as he spoke.

"Never know about that one, boy," replied Peter. "Last report we had on Blackbeard's crew was that he was hiding out somewhere near Puerto Rico. We have a full crew manned in the gun port and are prepared to handle them. Our best sailors are on watch up in the Crow's Nest on lookout. Besides, what pirate ship is going to take out us and the other merchant ships?"

His answer seemed to ease Jonathan's fears. Peter felt better knowing that he was able to be there for Jonathan.

"Well, I will seal myself in the trunk and cover my ears," said Jonathan.

Peter hugged him warmly. The seaman did his best to reassure the young boy that everything would be fine.

"I have my lucky locket with me," Jonathan told him confidently. "You know, the one that was with me when they found me on the steps of the House."

"Make sure that you keep that locket out of sight. It is special. There may be others who will try to use it for their own gain."

"Why, Peter?" asked Jonathan.

"You have a lot of questions, my boy. Maybe tonight or tomorrow night we will have a long talk. There are things I have been waiting to tell you. For now, I best tend to my duties. Relax, and I will see you soon. Remember what I told you about the other two seamen."

Jonathan had always sensed that Peter knew something about his past that he hadn't told him yet. He hoped their next conversation would reveal some new information.

"Not to worry," said Jonathan. "I am a survivor."

"Tell me about it kid," Peter said. "I have seen you survive that orphanage for some fifteen years. And I know all about surviving, my good buddy. I too was an orphan, raised on the docks."

Jonathan retreated to his trunk and closed the lid tightly. He held onto his lucky locket and thought about the stories Peter told him about the sirens.

Please watch over me mother. I know we will be together soon.

He opened the locket and held the silky lock of blonde hair between his fingers. He softly let it brush against his cheek. In that moment, felt closer to his mother than he ever had. He couldn't help but think about what Peter had said about his locket. There were so many things he still had to learn, but with Peter to guide him, he somehow didn't feel so alone.

Chapter 3

Hide for Your Life

Jonathan listened to Peter's footsteps as he walked slowly up the stairs. He knew the two other seamen would be down soon, so he needed to make a break for the head while he had the chance. He moved deftly in and out of the rum barrels and trunks, until he found a small room in the far back. He heard footsteps coming down the stairs just as he finished his business.

Drat! It must be those seamen coming to do their rounds. Oh, Please don't let them find me.

Jonathan felt an unforgiving wave of panic in his chest. He could feel his heart pounding through his entire body. He quickly hid behind one of the kegs of rum, holding his breath.

If they find me I will be made a Boatswain or worse, thrown off the ship!

A gruff voice broke the silence. "Hey Harold, what do ya say we check our rounds and then do some sampling of the rum?"

"Paulie, that's a sure way to get us mess hall duty."

"Yeah, we better not mess up. I need my Navy money for my family. You check the back rows of cargo and I'll take the front."

Jonathan mapped out a quick escape route in his head. If he moved from the keg, he could crawl on his hands and knees back to the head.

"Did you hear something, Paulie?" asked Harold.

"Just the sound of you licking your lips around all this rum," joked Paulie.

" Get smart, you old salt," said Harold.

Jonathan's heart was pounding. He hoped neither of them needed to use the head, or he would be toast!

He held onto his locket and prayed. As they continued, he became more certain that the seamen weren't doing a thorough search. He listened as they finished their duties and waited in silence until he heard their footsteps ascend the stairs.

As soon as Jonathan heard the cargo door slam shut, he quickly made a run for it. Knowing he was safe for a while, he sat outside of the chest and nibbled on some of the biscuits. He hoped Peter would return soon with a flask of water.

* * * * *

Suddenly, Jonathan heard a strange sound coming from behind the very front rows of chests. It sounded almost like something brushing up against wood. He hoped that it wasn't a leak. If it was, the rum it would soon flood the cargo hold entirely.

He crawled on his hands and knees around the corner of one of the crates. His heart pounded at the thought of someone coming down the stairs.

Jonathan could hear something coming closer. His heart was beating so fast again that it felt like it was about to explode out of his chest.

Then he heard the faint sound of a "meow." He saw a small cat round the corner of the keg. He sighed with relief. The cat came and rubbed its body against Jonathan's legs.

Although he was relieved to find it was just a cat, he was overcome with a strange sense of doom, along with the added superstition of bad luck ahead.

Seems I'm not the only stow away here!

The door to the cargo hold thrust open and Jonathan began to panic.

"It's me, Peter. I have water and meat.

Where are you, Jonathan?"

Jonathan called out to Peter as he was desperate for that food. They both sat against the trunk as Peter watched Jonathan chug down water and gobble down the meat pies that Peter had brought him.

"Thanks so much, Peter!" Jonathan said between bites of food.

"Peter, why is there a black cat wandering around down here?" asked Jonathan.

"That's another tale, my boy," answered Peter.

"What kind of tale?"

"Seamen say it is a warning of bad luck ahead. Legends even say that the cat isn't real."

"He's over there behind the kegs," confirmed Jonathan.

The two spent several minutes searching the cargo hold, but there was no sign of the cat.

"Sure, you weren't imagining things, boy?" asked Peter.

"I saw him," insisted Jonathan. He noticed that odd feeling returning again. He also noticed that he was beginning to feel light headed.

After a few minutes of silence, Jonathan spoke again.

"Soon I will be in Britain to search for my mom," he beamed with excitement.

Peter looked at him with empty eyes. "Jonathan, I hope you find her. I will do all I can to help."

"You know my story, don't you, Peter?" asked Jonathan.

"Yes, for the most part," Peter answered softly.

"Sister Mary Katherine told me that I was left on the steps of the Angelican House when I was just a few weeks old. I have searched through the records, but there is nothing other than that. Maybe you can tell me what you know. It will help me get closer to uncovering the truth."

Peter turned to Jonathan and placed one hand on his shoulder.

"I owe it to you, my boy. I have to go back up top and report for my other duty now, but I will come down in a few hours and we will have our talk."

Jonathan gave Peter a hug before he climbed back into the trunk. He kept wondering where the cat had gone. He was certain that he hadn't imagined it!

His thoughts wandered to the conversation he would soon have with Peter. He had waited his whole life to learn about how he came to be. It seemed that his waiting was nearly over. Jonathan drifted off to sleep with a smile on his face.

Chapter 4

Dead Men Do Tell Tales

"Aye, all will meet on the top deck starboard!" shouted Captain Lawford. "We are changing our course. We will head several points north toward the western end of Cuba and then through the Florida Straits. The seas will be rough, so batten down the hatches and all men secure your stations."

The men hurried to their posts. Thompson, a young seaman, had watch up in the crow's nest. It was his duty to keep a lookout for pirates and other nearby vessels. It also fell to him to stay abreast of the condition of the sea.

"Secure the main masts and the shrouds!" Lawford ordered.

Lawford was a seasoned captain with the British Royal Navy. He had been stationed in Jamaica since 1790. The navy knew he could commandeer this thirty-six gun frigate and lead a hefty convoy.

While Captain Lawford barked out orders on deck, Peter was looking after the cargo hold. He was grateful for his position, being able to keep Jonathan informed with the sea report.

As Peter looked up at the dark skies that lurked above the ship, a strange sense of doom ran through his body.

I hope I've done right by sneaking this boy on the ship, he thought.

Peter knew that he had to detain Paulie and Harold, the other seamen assigned to the cargo hold. Quickly, he worked out a scheme that he prayed would work.

Peter took hold of Paulie's arm. "Hey Paulie, the captain wants you and Harold to help man the gun port."

"Really?" Paulie asked, with gleam in his eyes. He had always wanted to get his hands on those weapons. "I'll go tell Harold."

Inwardly, Peter breathed a sigh of relief. He was thankful for the chance to check on Jonathan. There was something about the boy that made him feel fiercely protective. Despite the difficult childhood he had endured, Jonathan hadn't lost his sense of wonder and innocence. Peter hoped that he never would.

"Jonathan," Peter called softly into the cargo hold.

The moment Peter reached the bottom of the stairs, Jonathan had already rushed into his arms.

"Listen, Jonathan," he said quickly, urgency in his voice. "The captain just informed us we will be changing course due to the rough seas."

"How rough will they be?" inquired Jonathan.

"We should be okay Jonathan, don't worry," Peter reassured him. "I've been through some pretty turbulent waters before and lived to tell the tale. These ships are built strong. Let's go sit by your trunk for a while and have that talk."

They sat on the damp wooden floor in front of the trunk, their feet splayed in front of them. The room was dimly lit by a few lanterns that were swaying from the rafters. One had cast its glow right on Jonathan's trunk.

Peter turned to face Jonathan, but couldn't find the words to speak. It was difficult to know where to begin.

"What's wrong?" asked Jonathan.

"I'm just trying to think of where to start, my son."

Jonathan's eyes were as big as saucers. He looked expectantly at Peter, desperate to learn the secrets about his past that he had kept hidden for so many years.

"Let me say everything that I need to say. When I'm done, I will answer any of your questions, okay?" Peter said nervously. His trembling hands smoothed over his long grey hair.

"Your mother was a Hutchins. She was the daughter of Regis Hutchins, owner of the Hutchins Coffee Plantation. You should recognize the name, it is one of the biggest plantations in Jamaica."

Jonathan nodded his head, staying quiet.

"The family was also one of the richest. Her name was Julia. I remember hearing the fishermen talk about her like she was a princess - she was, in her daddy's eyes. She was such a beautiful girl, Jonathan.

She used to accompany the family's helpers to market to buy fresh fish. I was a young lad, but I remember seeing her like it was just yesterday. She was very tall, and had long dark blonde hair. It was the color of wheat, and cascaded all the way down her back. When she walked, those long curls would bounce up and down. I couldn't take my eyes off of those curls. Julia had eyes, the deepest shade of blue, just like yours. So often, I see her in your face…" Peter's sentence drifted off as he became completely consumed by her memory.

"She loved the tall ships and always would come aboard to explore. She fell in love with the son of a poor, local fisherman, Drake Belafonte.

Well, one thing led to another and she became pregnant when she was sixteen-years-old. She was a very smart girl. Her parents were about to send her off to England to attend a prestigious school. She ended up telling her parents that she planned to marry Drake. When her father found out, he was outraged. He told Julia that she could not marry Drake or keep the baby – you. She threatened to run away, but her father bound her to the house until she delivered the baby."

"She was a prisoner!" shouted Jonathan.

Peter put a hand on his shoulder to try and calm the poor boy down. "You were not left on the doorsteps of the orphanage. Mr. Hutchins had made plans before you were born, that you would go to the Angelican Home for Boys. Dalia, one of the family's helpers, cared for you in her room for six weeks. After that point, your grandfather signed the papers and took you to the orphanage. Your mother never got the chance to see or hold you."

Peter saw tears well up in those big blue eyes of Jonathan. "Are you okay, my son?" asked Peter.

"No, but I need to know," whimpered Jonathan. "Please continue," he said.

* * * * *

Suddenly, the ship rocked from side to side. "We must be just hitting a rough spot," said Peter. "Hang onto your trunk," ordered Peter. They could hear the pounding of feet up top. He knew that the men were busy trying to secure the masts. Peter did his best to block out what was happening above them, and continue with his confession.

"Right after you were delivered to the home, your mother was sent off to England. She attended school and lived with her aunt. I heard she remained there and became a school teacher."

"What became of my father, Drake?" asked Jonathan.

Once again the ship pitched from side to side. Peter put his arm around Jonathan. "Are you okay?"

"As okay as I can be," Jonathan replied.

"Rumor has it that Drake went out on a fishing trip shortly after, and never returned. There was a bad storm at sea and his boat was far too small to handle it. The boat was never found...nor was Drake. There are those who whisper and tell of a darker story. They say Mr. Hutchins paid someone a lot of money to kill him."

Jonathan sat quiet and still for a moment. "I want to believe that it was the storm that took him."

"Me too."

"So all that time I was at the Angelican House, none of the family came to see me?" Jonathan paused, remembering. "I do remember a large black woman who would come and help the Sisters cook. She would always seem to be looking at me. That was probably Dalia, the nanny who took care of me. It also explains why I got so many presents at Christmas.

Now it all makes sense," Jonathan continued. "I think I know now how I got my locket. Sister Katherine told me that a nice lady left it especially for me. I bet it was Dalia."

"You are very perceptive, my son," said Peter.

"And I bet Dalia is the one who put the lock of hair inside of it so that I had something of hers."

"You may be right. Jonathan, be careful with that locket. Your mother's family was wealthy. That locket is no doubt made from solid gold."

"Solid gold!" cried Jonathan. "I will treasure it always, not because it is gold, but because it belonged to my mother."

"Well, now you know the truth, my son. I know it is a lot to take in, but it was time to tell you."

"I am thankful that you did," Jonathan said. He leaned in and gave Peter a big hug. He was the closest thing to family that Jonathan had ever really had.

"We will look for her when we get to England. She should be about thirty-one-years old now."

"I hope she wants to see me," Jonathan said with a twinkle in his eye.

"Of course she will. You are a fine lad," said Peter.

CLANG, CLANG, CLANG, went the ship's bell loudly All men were needed on the top deck.

"I'll be back Jonathan. Get into the trunk, close the lid, and don't come out until I return," ordered Peter sternly.

They hugged once more before Peter hurried up the stairs to the top deck. He tried to ignore the sense of doom that felt heavy on his chest.

Chapter 5

The Wreck

All were on deck now, and orders were being given from all directions. It was a moonless night and the sea was as black as pitch. The sound of the waves thrashing against the ship rose above the yelling of the crew on the Convert.

It was now the wee hours of the morning, on February 8, 1794. Instead of the crew getting a good night's rest, their distress gun was fired.

Captain Lawford came bounding out of his quarters. Dressed in only his trousers, he raced barefoot onto the top deck.

"What in land's end is happening here? I heard the distress gun fire!" he cried.

"Aye, Captain, there be breakers ahead!" shouted seaman Thompson from up in the crow's nest. "The fleet is getting ahead of us now. They are all firing off their distress guns."

Lawford grabbed the telescope from the seaman standing next to him.

"Damn, this can't be the Grand Cayman reef! I thought we passed that an hour ago. I charted this course myself, so that we would avoid that bloody coral reef!"

He shouted orders for all of the men to report on the deck. Before any of the men had time to react, a voice alerted them to a whole new danger.

"Pirates - there be Pirates!" shouted men from the Britannia, which was close on their starboard side. All of the ships began to move closer, trying to protect the Convert.

The crew aboard the Convert flashed their lanterns. All they could see were ships clustered together…too close together.

They heard the sounds of the crash before they saw it. Splintering wood and screams of terror echoed over the water. It was as if the reef had sliced right through the ships, like an axe slicing through wood.

"Take cover, men!" shouted Captain Lawford, just before the Britannia rammed into the Convert.

When the ships collided, it hit the Convert hard into the windward reef. The ship began to lean on its' side, ready to split.

The remaining ships crashed into one another in an endless pile up. The deafening sound of screams mingled with bodies splashing into the water. Many of the seamen were now jumping into the water, clinging onto pieces of the ship that floated nearby.

"It is Poseidon coming to take us to our watery graves!" shouted one of the men in the water.

Despite the chaos, Captain Lawford still shouted out orders. They were largely ignored, since every man was out to save himself – all but one, of course. There was one seaman who had to save his dearest friend.

* * * * *

Dear God, please let me get down to Jonathan in time.

Peter did his best to hold onto anything he could to make his way down to the hold. The ship's hull had been hit hard and would be soon flooding with water.

Peter threw open the cargo door and raced down the steps. He was already knee deep in murky water. The trunks were swishing around, banging into one another.

"Jonathan! Jonathan, I'm coming!" Peter yelled, as he sloshed through the water.

Jonathan popped the lid of his trunk open and began yelling for Peter.

"Peter, what is happening?"

"We have hit the reef on Grand Cayman, Jonathan. All of the other ships have slammed into each other. We are all going down. You've got to get out of that trunk - now!"

"No, no…I'm afraid!" cried Jonathan. "I can't swim!"

"It doesn't matter now, my son. Just hang onto me and we'll grab a hold of whatever we can find until we are rescued."

As Jonathan tried to sit up, the chain of his locket got caught in the latch of the lid. He desperately tried to untangle it, but it had formed a small knot that refused to come undone.

Peter was still holding onto the trunk when a huge gush of water came and swept him away. He had been pulled down through the hold. Jonathan couldn't see exactly where he was, but there was a small crack that he could see out of.

"Peter! Peter, where are you?"

Jonathan prayed that Peter had been able to swim to safety. His trunk had begun to slam into all of the other trunks; he could feel water dripping onto his face. Jonathan pulled and pulled at the knot in the chain, but nothing worked. The more he pulled at the chain, the tighter it pulled around his throat.

Jonathan's body trembled, as he closed his eyes one last time.

I know I will be with you, mother. Please look after me.

* * * * *

As water overtook Jonathan's small body, his trunk was pulled through a gaping hole in the ship. His trunk landed at the bottom of the sea, nestled underneath a large crevasse deep under the reef.

A large sea turtle who happened to be in the area circled the chest. It seemed to take on an iridescent green glow that lit up the waters with its shimmering light.

Chapter 6

Grand Cayman 2012

"Mrs. Wallace, this is Mrs. Banks, deputy principal at Island High School. Your son, Brandon, did not show up at school today."

Mrs. Wallace paused a moment before answering. She knew exactly where her son was. "I'm sorry, Mrs. Banks, I believe I know where he is. I will call his father right now."

"Brandon has already missed nine unexcused days this year," scolded Mrs. Banks. "With his grades, he cannot afford to be missing so much school. Please bring him in tomorrow, along with your husband so that we can discuss the matter."

"Yes, ma'm," answered Mrs. Wallace, in a solemn voice.

* * * * *

Mrs. Wallace was already at work at Island Gems Jewelry and was not prepared to start her day in such a way.

As soon as Mrs. Wallace hung up the phone, she dialed her husband's work number. She dreaded telling him the news.

"Franklin, Brandon skipped school again."

"Damn that boy!" Mr. Wallace shouted in reply. "I can't leave the port right now."

Mr. Wallace had gotten a promotion to supervisor at the port a few years ago and spent most of his time at work or on call when he was at home. This is about the time Brandon had begun to have some behavior issues.

"You know where he is, Franklin."

I will talk to him tonight," confirmed Mr. Wallace.

"We need to do more than just talk," she said.

"He's a seventeen-year-old boy. He needs to be getting his act together. Trust me, Jenna, when I am done with him, he will know that I mean business!" said Mr. Wallace, angrily.

* * * * *

"Hey, Jason, did you see that spotted eel?" Brandon asked, excitedly, as they emerged from the sea.

"He must have been at least six feet long!" Jason answered.

They sat at the edge of the shore and removed their snorkeling gear. The early morning sun shone down and illuminated the crystal blue water. Brandon shook his head of dark wet curls, like a dog shaking out his wet fur. Jason on the other hand, was busy pulling back his sandy blonde hair into a printed scarf.

"I can't wait to get these pictures up on the computer and check them out," Brandon said. "Want to come up to the house?"

"I'd better not. I should get home and clean up before my folks find out I skipped school with you."

"Suit yourself," Brandon said as he walked away. He shook his head, knowing that Jason wouldn't get into trouble if he got caught. He wished his parents were as lenient as Jason's.

* * * * *

Brandon walked along the shore toward home. He gazed out at the turquoise waters, feeling the breeze on his face. As he kicked his toes through the white powdery sand and watched the palms swaying back and forth, he thought of his childhood. Brandon and his dad would go fishing and diving almost every weekend. That changed a few years ago when his dad had gotten the promotion. Brandon yearned for those days and hoped his dad would come around again. When he thought of those days, he knew that the sea was his heaven.

As he reached home he sat on the back deck of the large cottage and tried to take it all in.

He was grateful to live right on the beach where he could have the sea right there under his nose.

All of a sudden, Pirate, the family's five-year-old Labrador Retriever came bounding out and began licking the salt water off his face.

Brandon knew he had to get out of his gear fast and clean up before his parents got home or he'd have hell to pay.

Chapter 7

One Last Chance

Brandon sat at his computer desk admiring the underwater photos he had shot with Jason. As he studied one particularly striking photograph, he heard the garage door go up. He knew it was his dad coming home from work. He silently prayed that he wouldn't get caught for skipping school. When he heard the kitchen door slam as his dad walked inside, Brandon knew that he was done for. He listened to the heavy footsteps coming closer to his room.

"This is the last straw, I'm telling you, the last straw!" shouted Mr. Wallace as he burst into the room.

Brandon sat in silence at his desk, not even daring to look his raging father in the eye.

"Talk to me boy!"

More silence.

"You were snorkeling today, weren't you?"

Brandon looked at his dad with empty hazel eyes.

"I tell you, I have a notion to send you to your Aunt Linda's in Florida."

"No, dad, NO!" cried Brandon. "The island is my life! I would rather die than leave! I promise that I'll smarten up."

Mr. Wallace softened for a moment. "I've heard this before, son," he sighed. "You're better for a week or two and then it's back to the same old habits."

Brandon stared at his dad, who rested his hands on his head. He was a large man with broad shoulders and a well-built frame. He took pride in working out, though some of it was simply good genes. Brandon had inherited that same strong frame.

Mrs. Wallace appeared in the doorway with red, swollen eyes. That seemed to snap Brandon's father back into his fit of rage.

"See what you are doing to your mother, and this family?" shouted Mr. Wallace."

"In trouble again, flunky?" Brandon's younger sister, Murielle, shouted, as she walked toward her room. Her long black ponytail swung behind her as she strutted away.

Murielle was only ten but had it all together for her age. She earned top grades and excelled in sports. She made up for what Brandon had lacked in many areas. She was also the 'apple' of Mr. Wallace's eye.

"Smart ass!" Brandon shouted in return. He turned his attention back to his parents, who still stood authoritatively in his bedroom.

"We have an appointment with the school tomorrow," said Mrs. Wallace. She paused for a moment to collect herself. "Tell me you didn't go into the sea alone, Brandon."

"No, mom, I went with Jason."

Mrs. Wallace was relieved he did not go alone, as for the choice in friends-Jason would not have been her first pick. She knew he had a troubled past as Brandon had shared some of it, but believed he kept more of it to himself.

"You take after your grandfather, Kendricks, that's for sure. He lived for the sea."

Brandon had a moment of silence, as he remembered all the times he had spend fishing with his grandfather before he became ill. It was Grandpa Kendricks who first taught him to fish. It seems the two most important men in his life left him with only memories; one of them, had the ability to change that situation.

* * * * * *

The next morning, Mr. and Mrs. Wallace walked into the school with Brandon. Once they reached Mrs. Bank's office, Brandon could feel his heart start to thump in his chest. He hated when adults made his life their business. "Please, do come in," said Mrs. Banks in a pleasant tone. She was a large black woman who looked to be in her early thirties. "Let me introduce you to Mrs. Jenkins, our new counselor."

Mrs. Jenkins was very new to the school and had the reputation of being a tough cookie. She had her light blonde hair pulled up tight in a bun and wore a plain blue structured suit.

"Let me lay it right on the table," started Mrs. Banks. "Brandon is in serious trouble here. He has missed nine unexcused days of school this year. His grades are falling. If this continues, he may need to repeat his junior year."

Both Mr. and Mrs. Wallace sat in silence.

"Brandon, do you understand the serious nature of this situation?" Mrs. Banks asked.

"Yes, m'am, I do."

"Brandon, you will report to Mrs. Jenkins once a week, on Wednesday afternoons. You will have private counseling sessions with her until you show a notable improvement in your attendance."

"I will be in close contact with you, Mr. and Mrs. Wallace," Mrs. Jenkins added.

"We can't thank you enough for all that you are doing to help Brandon," said Mr. Wallace.

"You know, Brandon can turn this around if he puts his mind to it," Mrs. Banks said, earnestly.

Now that a plan had been set, the adults shook hands, and Brandon hurried down the hallway of Island High School to his first class.

* * * * *

"Hey Bran, heard you're in the doghouse again," one of his friends called out to him.

Brandon ignored him and headed straight for class. He handed Mr. Taft, his English teacher, the late note from the office and took the last seat in the back row of the classroom. He gazed out the window, taking in a view of the sea. Once again he was lost in the deep blue.

Chapter 8

Changes Ahead

Early the next morning, Brandon was up and ready for his fresh start at school. It was the last week of January and February was creeping steadily closer. He had already decided that February would be the month he would redeem himself.

His parents sat down with him over breakfast and reminded him that this was his last chance to pull himself together.

"You need to know how serious this is, son," said Mr. Wallace before he headed out the door.

"Hurry up with your breakfast, Brandon. I can't be late for work," said Mrs. Wallace. She was still in the process of curling her short black hair. She had always been a woman who took pride in her appearance. "You have a meeting with Mrs. Jenkins today, so don't be late. I'll call her later to make sure you had your session."

"Geez, I feel like a criminal," moaned Brandon.

With that, Mrs. Wallace, Murielle, and Brandon hopped into the car.

"Wait, wait!" shouted Brandon. "I need to run back in and grab my dive gear. Jason and I are supposed to dive off Cobalt Coast right after school."

"I don't think so, my dear," said Mrs. Wallace, "Your dad and I have decided to ground you from water sports for at least two weeks."

"No way!" Brandon shouted.

"We need to see that you are keeping up your side of the bargain."

Brandon stared out the car window in silence. Without the water, what did he really have?

He glared over at Murielle sitting in the back seat, despising her at this moment, as he knew his parents wanted him to be just like her. This only intensified his anger.

* * * * *

During lunchtime, Brandon sat with Jason and their friends Terrance and Blake in the outdoor cabana. They would all be seniors next year; well, if Brandon passed his classes this year, that was.

"Just wanted you to know we're here for you, Bran," said Terrance, as he put his arm around Brandon.

"How about we treat you to dinner tonight?" asked Blake.

Brandon looked away and replied sadly, "Isn't gonna happen."

Brandon and Jason had been friends since the seventh grade, but he had only known Terrance and Blake for a couple of years. They had moved to Cayman from England when their fathers' came to work at the banks.

"Well, guess you'll be out of commission for a while," said Jason with a smirk on his face.

"Guess so," Brandon muttered. "What happened with your parents?"

"Oh, they are cool with it," Jason boasted.

"Lucky you!" Brandon replied. "Hate to tell you this, but I won't be diving with you guys after school. I've been grounded from water sports for two weeks."

"You could always go over to Eva's house and study with her," teased Jason.

"Very funny."

His friends knew that Brandon had a crush on Eva Johnson. She was a pretty girl in his first period English class. Even though she was a girly girl who would hate going in the water and messing up her hair, Brandon always got flustered whenever she was around.

"We'll take some pictures and email them to you if we see anything cool," his friends chimed in as they tried to console him.

"Thanks, guys," said Brandon. He stared at his lunch - a meat patty and some apples. He didn't feel much like eating. "Guess I had better go, so I don't miss my appointment with Mrs. Jenkins," he said.

With that, he walked away from his friends and thought about everything he would be missing.

* * * * *

"Please, sit down and relax," said a smiling Mrs. Jenkins.

This was far from what Brandon had expected. All day long he had prepared himself for another angry, demanding adult. The last thing he had anticipated was a smile.

"This is your session folder, where I will take notes and report your progress to Principal Banks and your parents."

"Fine," said Brandon.

"Let's get started on today, Brandon," she said in an upbeat tone. "Tell me one thing that you like at school."

"Well, I enjoy science class and learning about sea life."

"That's good," she said. "See, you do have something that interests you."

"Well, my first love is the sea," he beamed.

"I was told that by your parents. You know, Brandon, if you study really hard and attend classes regularly, you could have a promising career in marine biology or something in that field," she said, encouragingly.

Brandon's eyes lit up.

"That would be great!"

"With good grades and hard work you could even earn a scholarship to a great college."

The two of them talked about what it would take for Brandon to one day turn his love of the sea into a career. After Mrs. Jenkins made some notes in his folder, he was dismissed.

He walked out the door to her office and decided that the first session he had so dreaded, hadn't been so bad.

* * * * *

Brandon waited in the parking lot for his mom to pick him up. He could see Terrance, Jason, and Blake loading diving gear into Blake's van. Just watching them get ready to head out made his body feel heavy with depression.

Then, a thought popped into his head. It tugged at his every breath, filling him equally with fear and exhilaration. He would sneak out at night and go snorkeling when his family was asleep.

His heart started to race as he pondered it. He started mapping out the finer details and considered the consequences if he were to be caught. Even though he knew there would be hell to pay, he didn't care. When it came to the sea, Brandon had no control.

Chapter 9

Strange Visitor

"Well, I have to say, I am very proud that you are making a positive change," announced Mr. Wallace that evening, as the family sat down to dinner. "Mrs. Jenkins phoned to tell us that your session went very well."

"It won't last," quipped Murielle.

Brandon finished his dinner of fresh Grouper and candied plantain. He tried to push away the guilt he felt amidst all the praise he was receiving from his family. He already knew that he would disappoint them…and if he followed through with his plan, it would be sooner rather than later.

With a guilty conscience, Brandon excused himself to do his homework. The second he reached the sanctuary of his bedroom, he turned on the computer to check his emails. He was desperate to see if there were any pictures from his friends from their dive earlier today.

No email. Brandon sighed.

He rushed through his English homework to prepare for his secret adventure that night. Exhausted from his reading, his head plopped down on his desk. He was fast asleep before he knew it.

* * * * *

Clang! Clang! Clang!

Off in the distance, a loud bell rang. Pirate barked anxiously. Brandon lifted his head from his desk, feeling muddled and confused.

What the heck?

He could hear loud screams and voices calling from a distance. He went to open the back window so that he could find out what was happening.

The noises were shrill and made Brandon's head pound. He couldn't quite make out what he heard, but it sounded like, "Reef ahead! Reef ahead!"

He could see a thick mist off of the sea, with a faint green glow coming from the water. Just as quickly as the noise had woken him, they seemed to dissipate. He decided to go outside to get a better view.

Outside, the thick mist was barely visible but the green glow could be seen faintly, about two miles out into the water.

He looked at his watch - it was only nine o'clock. He felt the urge to grab his gear and explore. It was as though something was calling out to him…and he couldn't understand why.

He ran back inside to grab his snorkeling gear and make sure that his family members were occupied. A quick check found that Murielle was asleep, his mother was in her room reading one of her favorite romance novels, and his dad was already asleep. He left Pirate in Murielle's room and closed the door to make sure that the dog wouldn't follow him.

*****

Brandon jumped straight into the water from the back deck. It felt cool against his skin. In front of him, he swore that he could see a beam of light underneath the water. It was as if he was being led somewhere…but by who? And where? As if someone or something could hear his thoughts, a large sea turtle came up behind him. It startled him for a minute, but he felt a strange connection with the creature.

This sea turtle was different than any he had ever seen. It was if it was communicating with him telepathically. He couldn't explain it, but he felt it. When his eyes met with the turtle's, he was certain this was no ordinary Cayman turtle.

So you want me to follow you, Brandon thought as he watched it swim. The turtle emitted a green glow from the center of his top shell.

The turtle led Brandon out far into the waters, toward the underwater glow. At times the turtle would circle around him playfully. As quickly as that playful mood had been felt, a solemn one took over. Somehow, the sea turtle was letting Brandon know that someone, or something, was waiting for him.

Brandon had been swimming for a long while and felt his body began to tire. Eventually, he knew that he needed to turn around and head back home. As he swam back, he noticed the sea turtle trailing at his back. When he finally reached home and pulled himself out of the water, though, the turtle was gone. Its' green glow had also disappeared.

Feeling very tired and worried about breaking his parents trust, Brandon snuck back into the house to shower and crawl into bed for the night.

When he woke up the next morning, he couldn't be certain if any of it had been real.

* * * * *

"You're quiet this morning," said Mrs. Wallace, as she drove Brandon to school. He kept going over the events of last night in his head. Had any of this really occurred? What did it all mean? His head was spinning.

"Mom, have you ever heard strange voices coming from the sea?"

"Not that I can say, but I have heard some old tales from the fishermen that gather off Public Beach. They like to tell tales of haunted ships and the ghosts of the men that were killed in the Wreck of the Ten Sails."

"Really?" Brandon's eyes lit up like fireballs.

"I don't believe any of that," Murielle piped in from the backseat.

"Well, they are just fish tales," said Mrs. Wallace. "Your Uncle Julian usually sits with the fishermen on Saturday nights. Your Grandpa Kendricks had his own stories to tell. It's too bad that he's not still around to share some of them with you."

Once Brandon was dropped off at school, his friends soon greeted him.

"Hey buddy, we had a great swim the other night. You were missed," Jason told him.

"Yeah, I'm sorry I missed it," scoffed Brandon.

"Well, as soon as your jail sentence is over you can join us," joked Blake.

Before Brandon could answer, Eva came up behind him, shoving him playfully.

"Hey, ya trying to kill me?" he teased. Brandon tried to ignore the way color had flushed to his cheeks.

"No, not yet. I was just wondering if you wanted to come to a party at my place on Friday night?"

"I'm grounded, so I'd have to ask…"

"Well, hope you can make it. There will be a DJ and everything!" she beamed.

It started to drizzle, and a gentle breeze picked up. Eva grabbed her umbrella and headed off to class.

While Eva walked away, he kept his eyes fixed on her tall, thin frame, and the long caramel hair that blew gently across her face. He only hoped that his parents would let him go to the party.

* * * * *

At lunchtime everyone had huddled under the cabanas as it had started to pour.

"Hey you guys, have you ever talked to the old fishermen out on Public Beach?" asked Brandon.

"What, and spend the night listening to a bunch of old guys' stories?" ranted Jason.

"No, seriously," said Brandon.

"If you want to go buddy, you're on your own," said Blake seriously. "Half of those men are so old they don't know what they are talking about anymore."

"I heard there have been ghost ship sightings and strange screams coming from the sea," Brandon told him.

"The only strange sights they see are after they have finished a bottle of rum," said Blake.

"Very funny," said Brandon.

Even without the support of his friends, Brandon was ready to get to the bottom of what had happened. He hoped that the old seamen could tell him their stories and help him understand the noises he had heard coming from the water. Trying to force those thoughts out of his head, Brandon walked quickly to his class.

* * * * *

A moment after he sat down in his English class, Brandon felt something tugging at his neck. It felt like he was being choked. His hand instinctively went to his throat, but there was nothing there. He could swear that he felt a rope or a chain pulling against his flesh. The feeling intensified and he tried not to panic outwardly. He struggled to make it through the class.

The second that the school bell rang, Brandon burst out of the classroom. He ran to the nearest restroom and studied his neck in the mirror. He could faintly see an outline of a small round circle in the center of his throat.

He rubbed the spot and felt it grown warm, almost burning his skin. As quickly as it had started to burn, the mark started to disappear.

Brandon shook his head, trying to make sense of what had been happening. It had to be stress…what else could it be?

Chapter 10

Reality Check

The next morning, Brandon's alarm clock went off. He reached over to turn it off, but knocked if off his nightstand instead. Pirate jumped on the bed, rousing him from his barely woken state. He got out of bed half dazed and confused. He was still locked in the strange dream he had last night.

As he tried to recall his dream, that choking sensation around his neck returned. He tried to ignore it by focusing on the dream he had.

He remembered having a hard time breathing and being pulled by a heavy chain far out to sea. Eva was in the dream. That was the good part.

She was swimming near the reef. He remembered how beautiful she looked when she swam, like a mermaid in the crystal clear waters. She wore the most beautiful golden pendant around her neck. It seemed to gleam brightly in the sunlight. A small school of Angel Fish circled her as she swam.

He could see her and could hear her calling out his name. All the while, he was at the bottom of the sea, unable to move. He remembered feeling cold as ice. He remembered the sound of his name being called out like an echo, becoming fainter and fainter with each passing moment. Then, everything went black as he woke up to the sound of his alarm.

* * * * *

He replayed the dream in his head over and over again. He went through his morning routine, quickly showering, getting dressed, and heading downstairs to eat a quick breakfast. Despite following his normal routine to a tee, nothing felt normal. Lately, everything seemed to be different – even his dreams.

"I had this really weird dream last night," Brandon said to his family, as they sat at the breakfast table.

"Did you dream you were in trouble again?" teased Murielle.

"Enough, Murielle. Brandon is trying very hard right now," Mrs. Wallace said. She turned to look at Brandon. "Want to tell me about it?"

"Well, maybe at dinner," he said. He paused for a moment, trying to find his nerve. "I did want to ask you….may I go to Eva Johnson's party tonight?"

"I'll have to ask your father. He's already left for work, but I will call him later," she replied.

"Please, can you do it now so I can tell her at school today?"

Mrs. Wallace sighed, but got up to make the call anyway. Brandon sat motionless, his nerves going into overdrive.

When Mrs. Wallace hung up the phone, the look on her face said it all.

"No, no!" shouted Brandon.

"Calm down, Brandon. Your dad thinks that you will learn from this. There will be lots of other parties for you in the future. Saturday, you can go to sit with the fishermen you were asking about. Your Uncle Julian can even pick you up and drive you home. It would be good for you to spend some time with your Uncle Julian. That man adores you. Besides we will know you are safe if you are with family."

"This is so unfair," Brandon fumed. Why didn't his parents understand how important going to Eva's party was to him? He was trying to be good after all…minus the late-night snorkeling. What was the point of even trying, if they still didn't let him have a life?

* * * * *

There was dead silence in the car ride on the way to school. This was unusual, especially with the always-chatty Murielle there.

Mrs. Wallace broke the silence with a curt "And what is wrong with your neck?"

Brandon had been tugging at his collar and rubbing his neck since they left the house. The choking sensation had gotten worse since he had woken up. He wasn't quite sure what to do about it. Surely no one would believe him…especially if he told them about his dream.

Brandon's head was not right today. He didn't want to go to school. The thought of ditching crossed his mind, but if he got caught it would cause him a major setback.

"It's fine," he mumbled. "I think I'm just getting a sore throat."

Brandon felt his pulse quicken as they reached the school. He now felt anxiety rush through him, knowing that he was being held captive by his parents and also another unseen force.

* * * * *

Brandon waited for Eva outside of their first class of the day. When he saw her approaching, he hung his head slightly and stopped her at the doorway.

"Just to let you know, I can't come to the party tonight," he mumbled.

"Oh, no! It won't be the same without you there."

"I just need to chill until this grounding period is over."

Eva nodded, sympathetically.

Jason stood behind Eva, listening to their conversation. Brandon couldn't help but notice that he seemed to be oddly amused by Brandon's own misery. He was already dreading lunchtime. The gang would certainly hound him for having to miss the party that night. The idea of eating alone for a day seemed oddly tempting.

Once Eva had walked into the classroom, Jason made his attack.

"Hey, Bran, going to be released from the chain gang tonight?" he teased.

Brandon stood silently for a moment. Those words took on a deeper meaning than Jason could understand.

"No, I won't be joining you guys for this one."

Jason walked right out of class, with Blake and Terrance trailing him. They patted Brandon on the back. They felt his pain and decided not to pour salt on the wound.

"We'll send you some pictures and keep you posted of the night," offered Terrance.

"Thanks guys," mumbled Brandon."

Brandon calmed down and walked back into class. Jason was whispering something to Eva. He had his hand on her shoulder.

"Aren't you supposed to be in biology class now, Jason?" asked Brandon in a harsh tone. Brandon felt his whole body tense up and become warm with anger.

Brandon saw clearly saw that one. He just let it go for now.

* * * * *

Brandon spent the rest of the school day scheming. He was determined to get in another secret dive. If he wasn't allowed to see his friends or go to Eva's party, he had to have something to keep him sane. A dive might be just the thing he needed.

He already had it all worked out. He would work on some of his studies, then try to get in some night snorkeling off East End again, once the family was asleep.

The idea of going out into the water again was the only thing keeping him sane. It felt good to have something special…something that was entirely his own…something that his parents couldn't take away from him.

In between planning his excursion, he thought about Saturday night. He was looking forward to listening to the tales from the fishermen, even if he did have to go with his uncle. He just knew that they would have answers for him.

Chapter 11

Secret Messages

It was almost time. Brandon anxiously checked his watch, desperate to sneak out of the house. It was just past nine o'clock.

Okay, I'll do the rounds and make sure everyone is occupied. Then it's just me and the water.

Sure enough, his mom had passed out in bed with a book in her hand. Dad was asleep right next to her, the newspaper folded over his hands. He walked down the hall and peeked into Murielle's room. She was still in there with her TV blaring, Pirate at her side.

Brandon walked back into his room, trying to be quiet. He checked his phone to see if any of the gang had sent him any pictures from the party. Of course there were none. He figured they were all too busy having fun to think of him.

He sighed, trying to focus on the adventure he was about to have, instead of what he was missing out on. He even tried to block out what Eva was up to. As he changed into his swimsuit, he was almost certain that he could hear those odd yelling sounds from a few nights before.

He opened his window, only to hear voices screaming from the distance. Just like before, he couldn't quite make out what they were saying. He could again see a thick eerie mist off in the distance, hanging ominously over the sea.

* * * * *

Once he was out on the deck, the voices grew fainter and fainter. He quickly decided to pile all of his gear into the nearby kayak and paddle out. This meant that he could get further out into the water than last time. He was determined to figure out where the noises were coming from.

He was about a mile off shore when he noticed a glowing green light circling the kayak. It was the same sea turtle from the other night! Brandon decided to suit up and drop the small anchor into the water.

As soon as he jumped in the water, the sea turtle met him face to face. Those same gleaming eyes transmitted the same signal straight into Brandon's mind. Brandon could sense the urgency in its message. It was coming through as 'Follow me to a place that needs you. Someone waits for you.'

Brandon let the turtle lead the way, as he swiftly followed. He could never remember being able to snorkel so fast. It was as if the turtle was pulling him along with an invisible cord. He glided along the water, taking in the creatures of the sea. He swam right through a large school of Trumpet Fish and even was in the company of a few Stingrays. He was all too aware of where he and the turtle were headed – the wreck site. There was no doubt in his mind.

Based on what he knew from previous dives with his dad, they were about twenty feet away from the wreck site. Even though he was physically exhausted, he was trailing behind the glowing light from the turtle as they cut through the dark waters.

Soon they approached a large area that also seemed to emit a faint green glow. The glow encompassed a large circular area. Brandon looked down below and could see very large pieces of the infamous 1794 wreck. He held his breath and followed the turtle down about twenty feet. It led him along the reef to a large area with a cavern underneath the reef. It was there that he could see parts of old wood that had since become home for hundreds of fish since the wreck. A large green eel peered out from beneath the rocks.

As he took in the sight before him, that strange sense of doom returned. The choking feeling also returned in full force. He could feel something tighten around his neck. Suddenly, his chest became heavy. He knew that he had to surface.

Up on the reef, he found a place where he could take a break. Standing on the reef was against the law, but he tried not to think about that. He noticed the turtle surface. It was as if it had come to make sure that he was okay.

Overhead, thunder boomed and flashes of lightning struck close to the site. It was a strange sort of lightning, because, as it struck the water it created static electricity and began sparking like fireworks. Brandon had never known any lightning like this before.

The need to return to the kayak became apparent. The turtle seemed to be responding to his feelings and encouraged him to turn back.

Brandon swiftly swam back to the kayak, and once again was aware of the turtle trailing him. He jumped into the kayak and removed his snorkeling gear.

As he peered over the side to rub the shell of his new found buddy, he found him swimming away. He somehow knew this would not be the last time he saw this strange sea turtle. Brandon used the last of his strength to get himself home. He hoped that he would make it home before the storm got worse, or his dad found out where he had been. He feared the latter more.

Just as he just made it to shore, the storm hit. The rain was coming down in sheets. Brandon quickly dragged the kayak up onto the shore and ran into the garage. He changed out of his gear and stashed it away before sneaking back into the house and into his room. He was sure to bring Pirate into his room, since he knew the poor dog was afraid of storms. After everything that had happened that night, it was nice to have some company, anyway.

Brandon wrapped himself in a thick blanket. He had a chill after being caught in the rain. As he lay in his bed, he felt like he was coming out of a weird sort of trance.

Was any of it real?

He had heard about people sleepwalking and leaving their houses at night…but he had been awake. He just couldn't figure out how a glowing sea turtle could possibly be real. His head was spinning with question after endless question. He wondered what or who was out there.

* * * * *

As he drifted off to sleep that night, he felt warm and safe. After everything that was happening, he couldn't figure out why. Just before he succumbed to a deep sleep, he visualized the sea turtle and that unforgettable green glow.

Chapter 12

Fish Tales

The plan was set. It was Saturday afternoon, and Brandon had just spoken to his Uncle Julian. That night, they would sit with them, and watch the sunset over the sea. He was looking forward to talking to the seamen, especially after what had happened on his excursion last night.

* * * * *

Now, Brandon sat in the living room with his parents. They kept congratulating Brandon for the hard work he had put in this week. Little did they know that he had been sneaking out of the house at night to go snorkeling. Guilt gnawed at his insides.

"I think you'll enjoy the company of your Uncle Julian and his friends tonight," stated Mrs. Wallace.

"And my friends aren't?" Brandon asked, sounding more hostile than he meant to.

"I'm just saying that they haven't been the best influence on you. They like to party too much, especially that Jason."

After hearing Jason's name come up, it struck a cord with Brandon, but he knew he had to let this one slide. He had other issues to deal with.

Brandon rolled his eyes dramatically. He was tired of his parents trying to run his life. First school, then diving…now they were even putting down his friends! He could feel his frustrations mounting with each passing day.

Damn, thought Brandon,I just don't know how long I can take this pressure.

Thoughts of running away played with his head but he knew it was not the answer. What was the worst of the two evils here? He wondered.

Brandon stomped off to his bedroom. He couldn't deal with his parents anymore. His timing had been perfect – just as he clicked his bedroom door shut, his cell phone rang. It was Jason.

"Hey, Bran, you missed a good one last night."

"What happened?" inquired Brandon.

"It got pretty wild! Eva and her friends took her dad's new jet skis without his permission and her friend Crystal wrecked one of them into their dock."

"Wow, I bet Mr. Johnson was in a rage!" said Brandon.

"No, he's got so much money, he can just buy another one," said Jason.

"Did anyone get hurt?" asked Brandon.

"Nope."

"Who was Eva with during the party?" Brandon asked.

"No one, she was just hanging with Jenna."

Brandon breathed a sigh of relief. He couldn't help but worry that maybe she had been with another guy. It was good to know that Jason hadn't tried to make a move on her. He had always suspected that maybe he liked Eva too.

"Anyway, just wondered if you're still going up to Public Beach tonight to party with the old guys," teased Jason.

"Yeah," Brandon replied.

"Let me know how many bottles of rum they end up having," joked Jason.

Brandon gave a half-hearted chuckle. He thought that Jason should be the last one to talk about too much rum, since he was the one who always had too much.

Jason continued, "The guys and I will just be hanging out at Smith's Cove. Have fun hanging out with the old guys."

* * * * *

Brandon could feel his friendship with Jason splintering. Deep down he knew that Jason had called just to rub it in that he'd missed the party last night. He always knew there was a darker side to Jason. They had been friends for such a long time, though. It would be hard to not have Jason in his life.

They both shared a love for the sea, however, Brandon was not about to share a love for the same girl.

* * * * *

By the time six o'clock rolled around, Brandon was feeling anxious. His Uncle Julian would be there any moment. Brandon was certain that tonight would be important. It was time for him to understand what had been happening – and why he was a part of it.

He heard a car horn honk from the driveway. Slipping on his flip-flops, he hurried out of the house to meet his uncle. Brandon hopped into his dusty red Jeep, and off they went.

* * * * *

"Well, Brandon," Uncle Julian started, "are you ready to hear some old fellas spin some tales tonight?"

"Actually, I am," said an interested Brandon.

"I was surprised to hear that you were interested in attending our little gathering."

"Well, I thought it was important to hear some of the old stories about the sea," Brandon answered.

As they pulled up into the small parking lot, they could see four men already sitting under the small pavilion.

"Okay, Brandon, here we go! Don't take any of this too seriously," Uncle Julian warned him.

They walked to the pavilion and were greeted by four men, who Uncle Julian introduced as Mr. Evan, Mr. Jed, Mr. Luther and Mr. Josiah.

"Good evening, my friends. This is my nephew, Brandon. He is going to join us tonight."

"Welcome," said the men sitting on the bench.

"Just sit and relax, boy," said Mr. Josiah.

He was easily the oldest man in the group, probably in his early eighties. He had lost most of his hair but still had a straggly beard. The other men all looked to be in their early seventies. They had all lived on the east end of the island and were raised by fishermen fathers. The sea was all they knew. Brandon could relate.

Brandon grabbed a cold soda from the cooler next to the bench, as Mr. Josiah began to tell of recent sightings of one of the ghost ships.

"I was sitting right there in the boat just off shore around seven o'clock and could see that blasted thick mist come in again."

Brandon fell silent as he listened closely. He was eager to hear the old man's story.

"Soon, as the mist cloud passed, I could see the faint image of the Ludlow, emerge. I just sat there, my eyes fixed, and waited to hear something. But there was nothing, and it disappeared just as it came."

"Wow, how did you know it was the Ludlow?" Brandon asked, wide-eyed.

"I've seen pictures of it all my life in history books and in the logs kept here at the Seaman's Association. I've seen this ship once before, while I was way out past the reef, fishing. I could hear faint voices in the distance of screaming and yelling.

All of a sudden I looked behind me and this huge transparent frigate comes right by me. I tell ya, I almost had a heart attack. I thought it was going to ram the boat. It passed right along the side of my little Boston Whaler. As soon as it passed it was encompassed by that strange mist again and disappeared." Mr. Josiah took a swig from a bottle of Jamaican Rum and pulled out a big Cuban cigar from his pocket.

"Well, I recall the last encounter I had was about a month ago, when Mr. Jed and myself were sitting in the backyard around nine o'clock. We spotted that odd green light out by the reef again," said Mr. Evan. "We decided to hop in the boat and check it out. As we got closer, we could see it was in the shape of a circle, just about thirty feet from where the actual wreck was. We stuck our hands in the water and it felt cool – cooler than it should. We drove around the circle with the boat, but soon it dissipated. When we looked in the water, we could see nothing."

"That is incredible!" cried Brandon. "Are there any explanations for these strange occurrences?"

"Well, let me tell you, my nephew," Uncle Julian began, "some believe these oddities are the result of the spirits from the 1794 wreck of the Ten Sails, making themselves known. Eight men lost their lives in the wreck. Local men rescued the surviving crew on the ships. Men boarded their boats and some even swam out to save them," Uncle Julian continued. "That is why Cayman is free of taxation - the King granted us free for the great deeds our ancestors provided."

Brandon was listening with full attention. He wondered if what he was dreaming and experiencing was tied to the spirits of those men from the wreck.

"How do they know how many men died?" inquired Brandon.

"There was a manifest for each ship. One was kept on the ship and one was kept at the port where they launched," answered Uncle Julian.

"So they know the names of those who perished?" said Brandon.

"Correct," replied Uncle Julian.

"Has anyone else had an experience with the ghost ships?" Brandon asked the other men.

"My nephew and his wife had a strange experience while diving last year," said Mr. Jed. "They were right in the area of where the Convert went down, when my nephew's wife, Glenny, felt something pulling her back. She was behind an old piece of wreckage under the reef. She recounts hearing moaning sounds coming from the site. Gregg, my nephew, knew something was wrong, so he came and pulled her away. She was so spooked by the experience that she said she is done with diving forever."

"How long has this been going on?" asked Brandon.

"Well, for the past two hundred years," said Uncle Julian.

"And what about you, uncle…any encounters yourself?"

"None that I can report of. I do know your grandpa had sworn he heard the clanging of a ship's bell many times, and even screams of seamen coming from the area. His house was right there on the beach by Gun Bay."

I wonder why I never heard those stories, Brandon thought out loud.

"Well, most of the people around these parts don't fancy ghost stories much," said Uncle Julian. "They've been touted as fish tales for years."

Brandon sat quietly for quite a while. He was not prepared to share his stories with the men, at least not yet.

Somehow, the night had flown by. It was already midnight! Brandon was shocked at how much he had enjoyed listening to the stories of the old men, especially given how much he related to them himself. The men all enjoyed having the company of a young man at their meeting. Brandon was glad to know that he was invited back whenever he wanted.

They drove home with the windows down. A light breeze brushed against his skin.

"I really had a great time tonight, thanks, Uncle Julian."

* * * * *

When Brandon got home, he swore that he could hear the sound of a conch shell horn, coming from the sea. He stood there for a moment. He heard the sound once more and then all was silent again. No green lights, no screams, no ghost ships. Maybe things were starting to get back to normal. He could only hope.

Chapter 13

Sweet Dreams

Brandon woke to a bright beam of sunlight pouring through his window. It was Sunday - that meant church and family dinner. Life on Grand Cayman was pretty simple, and it was that way for generations. The Caymanian people made sure it would stay that way. Tradition was very important to everyone on the island.

The whole family sat together in church that morning. Out of nowhere, Brandon began to feel warm, too warm. It felt like he was burning up. That choking feeling around his neck returned with full force and he tugged at his shirt collar desperately.

"What's wrong with you, son?" whispered Mr. Wallace.

"Just a sore throat," uttered Brandon.

It grew worse and worse until Brandon had to leave the church to get some air. He gasped for breath, ripping at his throat with his fingers, but it didn't go away.

"Brandon, are you okay?" asked Mrs. Wallace, who had followed him out of the church.

"I don't know, mom. I think I'm going through some sort of change, or depression, or something. I don't know what's happening to me. Maybe it's from all the pressure with this new monitoring program at school."

"It's not forever," reassured Mrs. Wallace. "You have one more week to prove yourself. After that, your father will lift the ban. You'll be back out in the water in no time. If you're okay, I'm going in to finish listening to the last sermon. You go inside and sit down, okay?"

Brandon followed behind his mother and headed for the church kitchen for some water. He hoped it would help calm him down at the very least.

As Brandon sat in the kitchen, his head swam with thoughts. Nothing made sense lately – not what was happening in the sea, his dreams, or that choking feeling that left him feeling helpless. Something strange was happening, but he was no closer to figuring out what.

It was then that he noticed some dusty old books on a bookshelf in the corner of the room. He decided to peruse them to see if he could find one that would keep him occupied until church let out.

There was one that caught his eye in a flash. It was called 'Night of Terror'. The book was the account of the famous shipwreck, as told by the ancestor of one of the seaman on the Convert. He started to read the first chapter and was so engrossed in it, that he completely lost track of time. His eyes started to feel heavy and weighted. It wasn't long until he was lying down on the bench in the kitchen, drifting off to sleep.

* * * * *

"Okay men, secure all posts. Rough seas ahead!" Captain Lawford bellowed.

Clang! Clang! The ship's bell tolled loudly. Men were running everywhere, as Brandon found himself standing on the quarterdeck of The Convert, just outside the Captain's quarters. It was as if no one noticed him. He tried talking to the seamen but no one looked directly at him or answered him when he spoke. He felt like a ghost.

"Hey Paulie, we better go check on our trunk in the hold," someone said to a younger seaman.

These two men were standing right behind Brandon. He decided to follow them down into the hold to escape the madness that was coming from the top deck.

Once below in the cargo hold, the first man ran to the back of the hold, straight to a trunk in the back row. It was nestled next to about eighty other trunks that all looked exactly the same. Brandon was closely trailing these two men and somehow they could not see him or were unaware of his presence.

"Damn, Harold, it's all still there!" shouted Paulie.

Brandon could see the trunk was filled to the brim with gold jewelry. There must have been dozens of pendants, rings and chains.

"We've got to secure this trunk much better," said Paulie. "We are headed for rough seas and we can't afford to lose our treasure."

Brandon wondered what on earth they were up to. He remembered from his reading that the ships were only supposed to have carried rum, cotton, and sugar.

These two must have smuggled these gems onto the ship somehow!

He watched them tie the trunk down with heavy rope.

"Okay, that should hold her," reassured Harold. Let's get back on top deck. We don't want to be too conspicuous down here."

The boat rocked back and forth violently. As Brandon followed the two men up top, he struggled to keep his balance. He could hear yelling coming from the man up in the crow's nest.

"Giant sea monster ahead! It's swallowing the other ships, captain!"

Brandon could see the ships behind The Convert being run aground into the blackened water of the night.

"It's Poseidon, come to take us to his kingdom!" yelled one of the seaman.

"All men take to your own destiny now. Do whatever you can to save yourself," proclaimed Captain Lawford.

Brandon felt his heart pounding with fear. He stood there helplessly as he watched the ships crashing into what he could only assume was the reef.

Not far from where he stood, a young sailor lost his footing and was tossed violently over the side of the ship. The sailor fell into the water with a loud crash, falling atop of the coral reef that had cut him into two pieces at the waist.

So much screaming was heard from the ships that it sounded like piercing ghouls in the night.

Brandon could see Paulie trying to grip onto the side of the foremast, as it rocked back and forth. Soon, it tipped and the young man lost his grip and fell into the murky waters.

Harold was running down into the hold to protect his precious trunk. Brandon questioned the man's actions, as there was little point in saving gold when the ship was sinking fast. Brandon followed the man.

The hold had taken on a lot of water by now and the sound of the ship splitting could be heard. Harold ran to grab onto the trunk. He held tightly onto the ropes with his bare hands.

Brandon tried to grab the man from behind but found himself frozen again. It was as if he didn't exist.

"My jewels, my jewels!" Harold cried out.

A loud ripping sound could be heard, as the hull split in half. All of the trunks ripped through the gaping hole in the ship, taking Harold with them.

Brandon was now floating in the water with all of the trunks. He gazed up at the sky, but noticed it was a night without stars in the sky. Overhead, there was just a deep blackness.

* * * * *

"Brandon, Brandon, wake up!" urged Mrs. Wallace. "Honey, the church service is over."

Brandon came out of his deep sleep slowly. He felt groggy and fought off lingering feelings of panic. His dream had felt so real…too real.

"Are you alright?" she asked.

"Yeah, just started reading and got really sleepy."

Brandon tucked the book into his jacket pocket. He needed to keep reading. Yet another strange dream had left him needing answers more than ever.

* * * * *

On the way home from church, Mrs. Wallace suggested that Brandon's grounding be lifted.

"It is now affecting his health. I think we have been too hard on him," she reasoned.

Mr. Wallace paused for a moment, considering the idea. "Okay, but don't give me a reason to regret this, or I won't be so generous in the future."

"You're gonna be sorry!" ranted Murielle.

Brandon felt like a prisoner who had just been released. He couldn't wait to call the guys to tell them. Mostly, he was excited to tell Eva.

As glad as he was no longer grounded, there was another feeling inside that was tugging at his heart.

It was a strong intuition that he was somehow part of some unfinished plan. If there was one, then what was it and whose was it?

Chapter 14

Nighttime Rendezvous

Now that Brandon was free from his grounding, he was anxious to have a little fun. He decided to call his friends and see if they had any plans for the night.

He phoned Eva first, only to reach her voicemail. This was disappointing. He ended up leaving a slightly awkward message on her machine, asking her to call him later.

Next, he tried phoning Blake, only to find out that he was sick at home. He then tried Terrance, who was having a late night dinner with his family since they had company visiting from out of town.

Jason was his last hope. Even with things not so great in terms of their friendship, he needed a break. Brandon was in luck, as Jason was free. They agreed to meet at Brandon's house at five o'clock.   Brandon hoped that hanging out today might get their friendship back on track. Things had felt strained for a while, but it all lingered under the surface. Nothing had been discussed or even acknowledged.

For the past couple of years, Jason had gotten involved with some troublemakers who were older than he was. He had begun drinking and making some bad choices. He had invited Brandon to some of his parties but couldn't understand it when Brandon did not want to enjoy the same things he did. It had put a definite strain on their friendship.

* * * * *

By the time it was five, Brandon was completely absorbed in his research. He had started to research the Wreck of the Ten Sails on his computer hours ago, and hadn't stopped since.

He was on a site that had different takes on the account. There was even one that claimed there was gold on board The Convert, just like in his dream.

"Hey, Bran, you really believe in all that stuff?" Jason had snuck up behind him and was reading over his shoulder.

"I don't know. I'm just interested in all that strange stuff."

"Whatever floats your boat, man," replied Jason.

Brandon's room was littered with papers. He had printed out lots of information on the facts written about the gold that was snuck onboard. Jason picked up a loose page and began reading some of the information.

"What do you think about going down the road to Public Beach to listen to the fishermens' tales?" Brandon suggested to a half-listening Jason. His suggestion seemed to snap him back to reality.

"I had hoped you were in the mood for some jet skiing or snorkeling," said Jason.

"Well, we can probably swing both if you're up for it," said Brandon.

Jason sighed and ran home to grab his gear, muttering about how weird his friend had become lately.

No sooner had Jason left Brandon's house, than his cell phone rang. It was Eva.

"Bran, I am so glad you are off your grounding! Want to come over tonight?" she asked.

Brandon cursed himself for not waiting longer to hear back from her. "I would love to but I made plans to hang out with Jason and talk to the local fishermen tonight."

"Wow, are you turning into an old man on me?" she teased.

Before their conversation ended, they made vague plans to hang out on another day. As Brandon hung up the phone, he stopped to think about the oddity of his decision. A week ago he would have dumped the old guys in a heartbeat to go see Eva. What had changed?

Brandon quickly gathered all the papers he had printed out and stacked them on his desk. This was the real reason he was going to Public Beach tonight. He needed to question the older men.

Jason had returned and was off to see the 'Geriatric Set', as he called them.

"Hey, Bran, can you keep this in the cooler for me for tonight?" He passed Brandon some cans of beer.

Brandon gave Jason a look. He had just gotten off of his grounding and now he was holding beer for his friend. This was sure to get them both in trouble if they were found out.

"Okay, but if we get caught, you're taking the heat, buddy."

"My dad doesn't care, anyway, he's too wrapped up with his new wife right now," Jason said nonchalantly.

Jason's parents had split when he was twelve and his dad had just remarried. Brandon thought this to be the core of Jason's problems.

Without another word, the guys set off on the jet skis. They had a blast flying across the water. It was as smooth as glass today. This was the first time in too long that Brandon's mind was free of all the oddities that had occurred. He was almost back to his old self.

They rode mostly side-by-side, until he noticed a big Hatteras fishing boat moving in their direction. He could see Jason speed off right into the direction of the boat.

Is he crazy? What could he be thinking?

Jason was too far out to hear Brandon screaming at him.

Is he blind or what?

He watched as Jason flew right in front of the boat before making a sharp turn. He then sped back toward Brandon.

"Are you insane!" shouted Brandon as soon as Jason got back in earshot. "What the hell got into you?"

"Just playing chicken," answered Jason.

"Yah, you are nuts, my friend!" Brandon knew Jason liked to live on the edge, but he had never seen him act so risky.

Before the boys knew it, it was nearing seven o'clock. It was time to head to Public Beach to join the fishermen for the night.

They rode right up to the shore, dismounted the jet skis and walked over to the cabana where the small group of men had gathered.

"Well look what the cat dragged in," muttered Uncle Julian.

"Glad you boys decided to join us," added Mr. Jed.

Brandon introduced Jason to all of the men. Mr. Josiah was looking inquisitively at Jason.

"Don't I know you from somewhere?" asked Mr. Josiah.

"I doubt it," snapped Jason. Brandon could sense there was tension brewing between them.

The boys sat under the cabana and listened intently as the men took turns telling some of their latest stories, and retelling the same stories of the strange and reoccurring events related to the Wreck of the Ten Sails. Jason of course thought this was a good excuse to chug a couple of beers.

Brandon was quick to chime in with his burning question about the gold he had dreamt about. "Ever hear of a claim that The Convert may have been carrying a trunk of gold jewels?" he asked.

Mr. Josiah was quick to answer that one. "In fact, I have, young man. I heard this carried down firsthand from an ancestor of one of the seaman on the ship. He claimed that he overheard two seamen talking about this very thing."

"So there really may be gold down there by the reef buried somewhere?" beamed Brandon.

"Never know," added Uncle Julian. "I know lots of divers over the years that have heard that story and have been down there searching for it."

"I heard that the trunks were all broken up. They hit the reef and split open, so their contents were spewed about the sea," added Mr. Jed. "There is the possibility that these jewels are spread out and buried further beyond the wreck."

Brandon had a bright look in his eyes. Even Jason had put down his beer. The idea of treasure hidden along the ocean floor was enough to grab his attention.

Mr. Evan stood to pull up his saggy jeans, as he stared out into the sea and called their attention to some lightning off in the distance.

"Ya know what lightning does for the spirits?" he asked. Brandon and Jason were all ears now. "The lightning emits energy, and spirits from the other side are able to cross over the 'veil' during a storm."

"And how do you know all of this?" inquired Jason.

"I've been around a long time and have seen many things I needed to find the answers to," he said.

All the men nodded their heads in agreement.

"If you want some real action, go out on a night like tonight and you just may get a glimpse from Cayman's tragic past," said Mr. Josiah.

The night was getting long and the lightning was moving in closer. The boys knew that they had to jet ski back to Brandon's, so they bid the others a good night.

On the way back, they heard the lightning crack and watched as it lit up the water. Brandon could see the static electricity spark as it hit the water. He would almost feel the electricity running through his body.

By the time he and Jason got back to shore, he felt relieved. The old seamen had made him more aware of the lightening and what it might mean. Could it actually help to explain what had been happening lately? It was all too much to take in.

His thoughts were scattered and varied, as he tried to connect the dots. Was there really gold out there? And what was the sea turtle leading him to? And why? None of it made sense to him anymore. He just wanted answers.

Chapter 15

Friendship, Love, and Lies

When Brandon woke the next morning, he decided to persuade Eva to accompany him on a secret dive that night. If anyone could be trusted to keep a secret, it was Eva. He needed to find out what was happening to him lately. It was becoming clear that he couldn't cope with it on his own anymore. Eva was the only person he could imagine helping him through it. He needed her by his side.

Deep inside he knew he had serious feelings for her. His keen intuition told him that someday she would be his wife.

Just before his first period class, Brandon went to find Eva. She was standing with her friends under the lunch cabana. He approached quickly, feeling the desperation welling up inside of him.

"Eva, I need to talk with you right now," said Brandon urgently.

"Okay, geez. Bran, why are you so upset?"

"Let's go over to the study room. I need to ask you something in private."

Once they were inside the study classroom, they took a seat in the far back. There were only two other students in the room at the time.

"Listen to me Eva, I need you to go night diving with me tonight," he whispered.

"Oh, I don't think so!" she protested.

"Trust me on this one. Some things have been happening to me lately…I have had some sort of 'enlightenment' you could say, about something buried under the reef where the Ten Sails wrecked."

"You, enlightened!" she crooned. "That's a good one."

"No, really! Let me show you this book I am reading. It's all about a lost trunk of gold that supposedly is out there somewhere."

"That book is pure fiction."

"I've also had strange dreams, Eva," he said. Brandon hesitated before telling her the rest. "I have even connected telepathically to a sea turtle."

"Okay, now I know for sure that you need to see a doctor. Shall I drag you over to the nurse?"

Brandon put his arm around her and she looked the other way to stare out the window.

"I trust you, Eva. I know this is going to be a find of a lifetime! I just want to share it with someone I… love."

"Love . . . love . . . you are telling me this now, after two years of a casual relationship!" she shouted at him in shock.

"I thought you had feelings for me too, but I wasn't sure."

She looked up at him bashfully. Her cheeks flushed a deep fuchsia.

"Of course I did," she answered shyly.

Brandon grinned widely. It looked like his luck was changing after all. Things in his life were finally getting back on track. He wasn't grounded and the girl of his dreams actually liked him back. Now there was just the matter of figuring out this shipwreck.

"So you could say we are a couple?" proposed Eva.

"I guess you could say so," confirmed Brandon. He gave her a big hug and a quick peck on the cheek.

Life was good. Until, Eva brought his head out of the clouds…

"Hey by the way, what is that red ring around your neck?" she asked.

"It's something I can't explain yet, Eva. I think it's related to all this weird stuff going on. I printed off all of this information on it….that's why I need your help. We'll meet up after school under the lunch cabana to make plans," said Brandon.

"Well, I have to come up with some phony story to get out of the house tonight. They would never let me go night diving as they know I am not a good diver."

"You don't have to worry. I'll be there with you, and I am a pro."

The bell rang and Brandon was forced to run to English class. If he was late, there would be hell to pay with Mrs. Banks and Mrs. Jenkins. While Brandon rushed off to his class, Eva slicked her long caramel locks into a high ponytail, grabbed her purse and left the study classroom, not realizing that Brandon's research papers had been left behind.

* * * * *

All day, Brandon could think of nothing but tonight's adventure. It seemed that the whole morning blew by in a daze.

"Hey Bran, come and join us!" called Terrance and Blake at lunchtime.

Brandon joined the guys at their usual lunch table.

"Where's Jason?" he inquired.

"Don't know," said Blake. "We haven't seen him all day. Maybe he stayed home sick today."

Brandon woofed down his lunch - curry chicken - and grabbed his backpack. He made a beeline for his appointment with Mrs. Jenkins. Since things had been going so well for the last week, they wouldn't have to meet quite so often.

"Well, it seems as though we'll be meeting a lot less frequently, Brandon," Mrs. Jenkins said in a happy voice. "You should be just fine as long as you don't mess up again. Pretty soon, you won't have to see me at all anymore!"

With that, Mrs. Jenkins had him sign his chart and gave him a big hug. That had been their easiest session yet. It was nothing but encouragement and praise. Brandon just wished that he felt more worthy of it. Once he had figured out this whole shipwreck mystery, he vowed to stay on track – no more sneaking out, and no more being irresponsible.

As he left the office, he ran straight into Eva.

"Hey, did you have a chance to look at any of the material I left for you?" he asked.

"Oh my gosh!" she cried. "I think I left it in the study classroom. I'll run back to grab it right now."

"I'm coming with you!" he said in a panicky voice.

When they returned to the study room, there was no sign of the material. They looked all over the room and it was nowhere to be found.

"Oh no!" Brandon wailed. "I really don't want that kind of material just floating around the school."

"I'll run over to lost and found right now," she offered.

"I'll wait for you outside," said Brandon.

Brandon was sitting on a bench outside the school, nervously waiting for Eva to return. That was when he spotted Jason walking across the parking lot toward his brother's car.

"Hey Jason!" he yelled out.

Jason didn't even look at him, though Brandon was certain that he had heard him.

Just then Terrance and Blake came by to ask if he wanted to go to a party that night at the Beach Club.

"No, but thanks, anyway. I have lots of homework to catch up on," he said.

"Really, Bran? You could come up with a better one than that."

"Sorry guys. By the way, I just saw Jason. I thought he wasn't here today?" informed Brandon.

"Yeah, we thought so too, but Blake saw him outside the snack cabana reading a bunch of papers," said Terrance.

Brandon got a sudden cold look in his eyes. He felt his stomach drop as he pieced it together.

"You, okay, Bran?" asked Blake.

"Yeah, just thinking."

"Well, if you change your mind about tonight, you know where we'll be."

Eva raced out of the school but held no papers in her hand.

"Not in lost and found," she said.

"Not going to be there anyway," he fumed.

"What do you mean?"

"I think I know exactly where they are. Sometimes you can't even trust your closest friends," he said angrily.

Things between Brandon and Jason had been brewing for a while, but this was the last straw. He knew that the only reason Jason wanted those papers was so that he could try and get his hands on some gold. His selfishness was truly beginning to shine through the façade.

"Are we really doing this tonight?" Eva asked nervously.

"We have to. Now more than ever."

"Oh, Bran, do you really understand the consequences if you get caught?" stressed Eva.

"We won't get caught," he said reassuringly. "I promise."

Chapter 16

Dangerous Dive

Brandon eagerly awaited the arrival of his mom after school had ended. There was so much to do before his dive with Eva that night.

Damn, where is she?

He stood up with his hands on his hips as he gazed down the long school parking lot.

After what felt like forever, he could see mom's black Land Rover pull up. Murielle and her friend Janisha were sitting happily in the backseat.

"Sorry I'm late, honey. I had to wait on Janisha to get her things. She will be staying over tonight." Mrs. Wallace said.

Oh great – just what I need – another obstacle.

"Have a good day, Brandon?" inquired Mrs. Wallace.

"Sure did," he answered distractedly.

He knew that his day was only just beginning. He still needed to sneak out of the house in his dad's Jeep to get his rental tank from Diver's Delights. How he would do this was yet to become clear to him.

As soon as they got home, Murielle and Janisha ran up to her bedroom, giggling joyfully. Mrs. Wallace headed to the kitchen to start dinner.

"Hey mom, I have a great idea!" voiced Brandon. "Since Murielle is having a sleepover tonight, why don't we order pizza?"

"You know, that is a great idea," Mrs. Wallace agreed.

"Mom, just phone in the order to Island's Best and I will go pick it up in dad's Jeep," Brandon cleverly suggested.

"I think if your dad found out about that, he'd kill us both!" she joked.

"Come on, mom I've taken the Jeep out before," he reminded her.

"Well, okay…" she agreed hesitantly.

"Phone in the order and I'll leave to go pick it up. Come on, Pirate, old buddy, you can come too."

Brandon was amazed at his own quick thinking. It wasn't long until he was leaving the house to rent his tank before grabbing the pizza order.

* * * * *

"Who's your dive buddy, Bran?" asked Derek Burton, the man who ran the dive shop.

"Eva Johnson, but she is renting one from the Beach Club Dive Shop." Wouldn't think twice about going down there alone," he blubbered.

"Leave me your dive card, sign and date the receipt, and then you're done."

"Tell me again what the date is," asked Brandon.

"It is February 8th,"replied Derek.

Pirate started barking his head off from the Jeep.

"Okay, I hear you!" yelled Brandon.

He set the tank in the back of the jeep and covered it up with a large canvas cover. As he placed the copy of the receipt of the rental tank in his pocket he stared at the date.

No! This can't be real!

He realized in amazement that today was the date the Wreck of the Ten Sails happened, some two hundred and eighteen years earlier.

This is no coincidence.

His mind reeled at the anniversary of the shipwreck. Surely this had to mean something. Tonight was the night, he was sure of it.

As he drove up to the pizza shop a strange feeling came over him, as if he was back in the dream he had that day at the church. He felt dizzy and had to pull the Jeep over for a few minutes at the side of the road. It took several long minutes before the feeling passed and he felt okay to drive again.

By the time he got home, it was five o'clock. He only had four hours left until the big dive. His heart pounded with excitement.

* * * * *

"Pizza, delivery!" Brandon shouted as he bounded through the door. He slammed the two large pepperoni pizzas down on the countertop, grabbed two big slices and ran up to his room to begin his research for the night.

Brandon returned to several of the websites he had originally found about the legends of the wreck and the tales of the gold. He printed them off again to read while he gobbled down a slice of pizza. Pirate was there too, the Crumb Master that he was.

The next time Brandon looked at the clock, it was eight thirty. Time had a way of zooming by once he got reading.

Murielle and Janisha were busy watching movies in the bedroom, mom was already in bed with another one of her romance novels, and dad was downstairs watching a fishing show on TV.

Brandon knew that he had to get outside and load up the kayak with his dive gear as quietly as he could. Eva would be there in half an hour.

Brandon looked out the window. It was already dark and he could see heavy clouds looming. Once he had everything ready, he waited outside for Eva.

Where the hell are you, Eva?

At nine fifteen, a car pulled up. Brandon ran to meet Eva and help her unload her gear. They quietly carried all her gear to the back deck and set it in the kayak along with Brandon's.

"Okay, now here's the plan," Brandon started seriously. "I will run into the house to tell my family that I am hanging out with Blake and Terrance tonight. Then we take off in the kayak and row down to the beach a bit farther south. We'll beach the kayak, assemble and connect up all our dive equipment, and then row out to the site."

"Gosh, Bran, you've got this nailed down to a tee. I still don't understand why we need to do this,"

"Neither do I," Brandon replied.

* * * * *

Brandon and Eva paddled down alongside the shoreline of east end, down to a small patch of beach. They dragged the kayak up onto the sand and got ready to suit up.

"Hey, Eva, want to know something strange?" asked Brandon.

"You mean stranger than this escapade?" she joked.

"Tonight will mark the anniversary of the sinking of the Wreck."

"Did you know that before you asked me?"

"Honestly, Eva, I swear I didn't! It must be some weird sort of fate that we are out here on this date."

Now that the two of them were suited up and their equipment was ready to go, They loaded up the dive equipment and pushed the kayak back into the water. After they pushed it out a few feet they quickly jumped back in.

A squall was approaching, as the sound of thunder boomed in the distance.

"I don't know, Bran, maybe we should turn around and do this another time," pleaded Eva.

"We will be fine. It should pass us right by," he said. "You know how these island storms go. By the way, if a large sea turtle comes along, don't be alarmed, Eva, as it is just the telepathic old turtle I was telling you about."

"I actually think you might be crazy. I might be too for coming with you tonight," she replied, looking at him oddly.

They paddled out to the reef, where the water became choppy.

"Okay, Eva, we are dropping anchor here." he ordered. "We'll swim out about one hundred yards before we drop down. We are headed to a spot beyond the reef. That's where I think an old trunk got buried under a large crevasse."

"And you think it's still going to be there?" she enquired.

"Yes. I know there is something out there," he said confidently.

In no time, they were both in the sea, swimming just out beyond the reef. As they looked up to the night sky, they could see a huge dark cloud blanket the area just above the wreck site. It was the weirdest cloud either of them had ever seen. Streaks of lightning would flash in and out of it, but not come down and touch the water. They were short, jagged and spear shaped bolts that took on a weird neon glow.

It was time to dive. Brandon's heart filled with anticipation for what may lie ahead.

Soon they were about seven feet down and found themselves surrounded by a school of Sergeant

Majors. The light from their flashlights beamed ahead to reveal a very large spotted Grouper.

Brandon could see that Eva had started to calm down. He met her beautiful hazel eyes with his. Even behind her mask, she seemed calmer.

They descended another five feet before they held their noses and blew to equalize. They began swimming toward the odd green light that illuminated the sea up ahead. Eva swam right behind Brandon.

Somehow, Brandon seemed to know exactly where he wanted to go. He kept searching for his sea turtle friend and could not understand why he wasn't there yet.

Then, a light came from behind them. It wasn't the iridescent green glow Brandon had been waiting for, but the unmistakable light from a flashlight. That meant only one thing – another diver.

The diver pushed Eva aside and headed straight for Brandon. Eva was frozen in fear, unable to help. She saw that the other diver carried a spear gun, but the young girl didn't know quite what to do.

Before she could decide what to do, the diver had shot the spear gun. Brandon, swimming ahead still, was busy trying to reach their destination. Suddenly he felt a sharp pain rip through his leg.

He shined his flashlight onto his leg as he tried to figure out what had happened. The pain seared through his body.

He saw a light coming toward him and saw that it was another diver. Eva's tiny body lingered further back. The diver was only five feet away and was moving quickly toward him. Brandon panicked, unsure of what to do next.

As the diver got closer, he realized with a shock that it was Jason. His friend...his friend had just shot him with a spear gun! He couldn't wrap his mind around it. It was then that Jason reached out and ripped off Brandon's mask. He grappled for the mask as Eva surfaced and Jason swam ahead, looking for the treasure he hoped to claim as his own.

Brandon pulled the mask back over his face and blew air through the nose to clear it. He looked down to see his calf studded with a spear. Instinctively, he yanked it out, which caused an intense wave of pain to wash over him. It was clear that he was in no shape to go after Jason.

From the darkness of the water, he saw a bright luminous green light. Suddenly, his entire body was consumed with calm. His friend, the sea turtle, now faced him. Those ancient eyes locked onto Brandon's – he now knew that everything would be fine.

The turtle began circling his body. It emitted a neon green light, which encapsulated Brandon's entire body as if to wrap it in some sort of cocoon.

The sea turtle sent Brandon a telepathic message that it would swim with Eva until she surfaced and returned to the kayak. He watched as the sea turtle led Eva back to safety.

Brandon was still in the water. He stayed wrapped in the cocoon, waiting for the sea turtles' return. Up ahead, he couldn't see where Jason was. He assumed that he had already made it to the site.

Eva shined her light out onto the sea and she could see ahead Jason emerging out by the shallow part of the reef and lying there to take rest. He probably ran short on air and had to surface. Maybe the storm would get him before Brandon did, she thought.

Brandon was left to think about what had happened.

That rat. He snooped the gold story and wanted to find it himself, at the expense of hurting Eva and me.

Brandon could see the turtle returning to him, as he floated in his cocoon of thick green light. When it got closer, he knew that he could remove his mask and regulator, and breathe on his own in the water. It seemed impossible, but he knew to trust this underwater friend.

Meanwhile, above the water, the large storm cloud was flashing lightning strikes madly. They hit the water, creating sparks that lit up every place they struck. They came every few minutes, like a fireworks show. Loud screams could be heard from up ahead.

* * * * *

Brandon's eyes met the turtle's once again. He now knew that the turtle had been there at the time of the wreck on this day in 1794. He also learned through their telepathic communication, that the sea turtle's name was Mallock.

He knew that he needed to follow Mallock to find what awaited him. Brandon was sure it would be the legendary gold from the shipwreck.

They swam side by side, led by the glowing green light. Brandon had never felt so free as he glided through the waters along with Mallock and the schools of fish.

Above the waters, a faint image of an old sailing ship emerged. It was The Convert, moving eerily along the reef. There appeared to be no one on board, but the screams of the seamen grew louder and louder.

Giant lightning rods struck down on the reef with rage. Something big was brewing.

* * * * *

Eva sat up in the kayak amidst a blackened sea. She wrapped a blanket around her as she shook with chills. She could see a thick grey fog plowing through the wreck site as it seemed to carry the screams along with it, as if all the lost souls who had lost their lives were trapped in the mist. I pray Brandon will survive this night, she thought. How could I have doubted him?

She watched as giant lightning rods struck down to the reef with rage. She knew she was witnessing some paranormal event. As she shined her light over to the reef where she last spotted Jason, she could find no sign of him.

Chapter 17

Souls Lost, Souls Found

Brandon kept close by the turtle. He had hoped that Mallock was leading him to find the legendary gold he had so hoped to find, but instead was getting an entirely different feeling.

Mallock relayed the story of Jonathan Palmer. He learned the story of the young boy, whose locket caused him to get stuck in the trunk he had stowed away inside. Mallock shared that Jonathan's spirit was not able to fully cross over, as he was still tied to his tragic death at sea. His soul stayed forever trapped in that chest, until the locket was released.

Brandon now understood the call for help. It had been Jonathan who had been reaching out to him. He knew that it rested on him to release poor Jonathan's spirit. The choking feeling around his neck…the strange dreams…it all made sense now; He had been experiencing what Jonathan had just before he died.

Mallock locked eyes with Brandon once more as they swam about one hundred yards over the reef toward a large wall jutted with bright purple coral. A school of Bermuda fish and small blue fish peppered the sea around them.

A thick fog hung over the wreck site. The screaming continued, getting louder and louder with every passing minute. Out of the fog emerged another giant monolith of an old frigate ship. It was The Moorhall. The image was transparent and no men could be seen on board. This time, the sound of splintering wood could be heard as it crashed on the reef. A loud bell clanged, ringing through the night air.

The storm appeared to be gaining strength as another cloud was moving forward. This one was shooting its arsenal of lightning rods upon the water.

* * * * *

Brandon followed Mallock as they swam toward a bright neon light that was coming from ahead. As they approached the wall, they went down under a ledge that led to a huge crevasse. Mallock let Brandon know that he would need to go down alone into the small cave.

Brandon slipped through the small entrance to the cave. He could see what appeared to be a large piece of metal. It looked like a lid to a very old trunk. This was it! His keen intuition told him. The lid was covered in barnacles and other sea life. The neon light became more intense the closer that he got to it.

Brandon's hand touched the old lid. He could see an old rusted chain wrapped around the lock to the lid. When he reached out to touch it, his hand grew very warm and a vibrant golden aura circled his hand.

What on earth?

He examined this oddity with great interest.

Even though Mallock was behind him, he could still feel his messages. These ones made his heart sad, for he knew this was the chain to the locket that belonged to Jonathan. Brandon was overcome with an unbearable sadness as he thought of the young boy who lost his life.

Brandon could see the old tarnished locket at the end of the chain. He didn't want to pull too tightly on the chain. He wanted to keep the locket attached to the chain, but knew it had to come off of the lock at whatever cost.

As he gently tried to untangle this rusted chain, he was taken over by images of the last few days of Jonathan's journey. It was overwhelming for Brandon to take in. He couldn't imagine experiencing anything like what Jonathan had. He suddenly felt grateful for the life he had, and for his loving family.

Finally, with a few more yanks, the chain was untangled. He was able to retrieve the chain and the locket. At that moment, his body was pushed back a few feet by a strange energy. He watched a faint image of a young boy emerge from the site. It had to be Jonathan.

Brandon held the locket in his hand. As Jonathan's spirit floated toward him, he reached out and handed the locket to the spirit. It emitted a strong white light from his body as he took it. The light shone so brightly that it almost blinded Brandon. The spirit smiled as he held the locket before thankfully waving at Brandon.

Brandon was now receiving messages from Jonathan.

Thank you, my friend. I have been waiting for over two hundred years for you. I can finally join my mother and Peter. We share a 'divine connection'. Someday we will meet again.

Quickly Jonathan's spirit was swirling in a white cloud that rose up and out of the sea, leaving a faint white trail in its wake.

Brandon's feeling of sadness was soon overcome with joy. He knew that he had released Jonathan's soul – one that had been trapped in the water since 1794.

With that, Brandon swam out of the small cave to find Mallock waiting for him. As their eyes met, they both knew their mission had come to an end.

Will I ever meet you again? Brandon relayed to Mallock.

He did not like the answer. Mallock's mission was over now, and it was time for him to return home. Mallock had been Jonathan's protector. He wasn't needed in these waters anymore.

Mallock then told Brandon that he would always be offered safety from the sea for his selfless gift to Jonathan.

"I am thankful for this special gift," proclaimed Brandon earnestly.

It meant more to him than all of the gold in the world.

He returned to a very relieved Eva in the kayak. Pulling his body into the boat, he hugged her tightly. They both looked over the edge of the kayak and saw a faint trail of his green light, which grew fainter and fainter in the distance before disappearing altogether.

"I can't believe he's gone," lamented Brandon.

"I can't believe any of this," returned Eva.

"Well, where is the gold?" she asked.

"There was no gold, Eva."

"No gold? Then what was that mysterious turtle leading you to, and what were you doing down there for so long?"

"It's a long and unbelievable story, Eva. Let's get to the shore. I'll explain everything then."

The two headed back to shore. As they made their way back, Brandon noticed that the storm clouds had passed, but something even stranger had appeared. Although it was still dark out, a large cloud cover illuminated a golden glow directly above the wreck site. Beams of light replaced the lightning as they gently touched down to the reef, shining like millions of glittering stars upon the sea.

The heavenly glow seemed to fade just as quickly as it had come. The sea was now as calm as glass, which was quite a change from its raging white caps a few hours ago.

When they got to the shore, Brandon and Eva collapsed on the beach together. Neither one could fully take in what had happened yet; all they could think about was how exhausted they were. Brandon looked at Eva and put his cold arm around hers, staring into the safety of those familiar hazel eyes.

"Well, Bran, do you think anyone will buy our story?"

"They don't have to buy it, Eva, it is what it is – our story," he announced.

"So ya ever going to tell me what happened down there, Bran?" she asked.

"Maybe someday, Eva, but not now."

"And what about Jason? Where did he go?"

"I think the only one who can answer that is Mallock, and he is gone," Brandon sadly replied.

They both watched the sun come up over the sea, showing off its golden beauty, as it warmed up the crystal clear waters and gave birth to a brand new day.

Thank You for purchasing Jonathan's Locket. If you enjoyed it please leave a review for the author on Amazon.

You can also visit Lorraine Carey on her website to view more of her work.

www.lorrainecarey.com

Thank You!

CPSIA information can be obtained
at www.ICGtesting.com
Printed in the USA
LVOW10s1859100717
540844LV00011B/1331/P